"How about that castle?" asked Mr. Stein. "It looks nice."

"Oh, you won't like it," replied Mr. Flannel with a shudder. "Nobody likes that castle."

"Let's go and see it now," decided Mrs. Stein.

The Stein family peered through the rusty gates of the old castle.
Mr. Flannel had a creepy feeling that they were being watched.

"It does need a fresh coat of paint to brighten it up," he stuttered.
"Oh no, it's fine," replied Mrs. Stein. "Let's look inside."

"What a magnificent hall," commented Mr. Stein.

"And it's complete with wall-to-wall cobwebs—er, carpets," added his wife cheerfully.

But Mr. Flannel wasn't listening. He had seen something hiding in the corner—something **very spooky.**

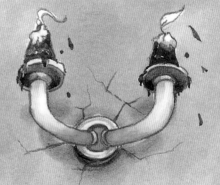

Next, they went
to look upstairs.
"The bedroom is a little
breezy," said Mr. Flannel,
trying not to shudder as he
looked out of the window.

"But a new pair of
curtains will make a big
difference," added
Mrs. Stein. All her
husband could say was
"Lovely view!"

Mr. Flannel was beginning
to think that the Steins
were a little odd.

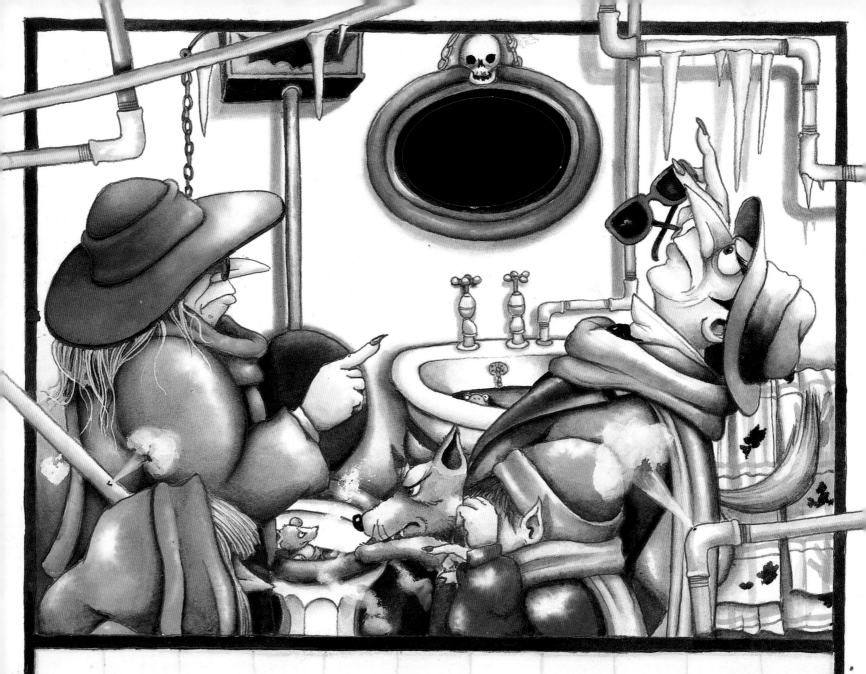

"The bathroom does need some work," agreed Mrs. Stein as her husband inspected the icicles hanging from the pipes.

But Mr. Flannel was busy staring at the bathtub
—there was someone still in it!

Mr. Flannel led the way down the steep, slippery steps to the cellar. "This cellar is very damp," he said, sneezing loudly as they gazed into the murky depths below.

Danny's eyes nearly **popped** out of his head! Something down there was moving—
something very big and slimy!